BLINK OF
AN EYE

DAVE,
THANKS FOR EVERYTHING.
ESPECIALLY SHARING JULES
WITH ME WHEN SHE GETS LONELY.
LOVE HER MORE EVERY WEEKEND
SHE SPENDS WITH ME.

David J. Karaffa

the Peppertree Press
Sarasota, Florida

For information regarding permission,
call 941-922-2662 or contact us at our website:
www.peppertreepublishing.com or write to:
the Peppertree Press, LLC.
Attention: Publisher
1269 First Street, Suite 7
Sarasota, Florida 34236

ISBN: 978-1-61493-589-6

Library of Congress Number: 2018905210

Printed June 2018

This was passed down from an old Bahamian elder while in the Bahamas. It was given to share and it holds true to life about being responsible for your own actions. So I'm sharing it in hopes it helps others in their daily lives.

I am who I am for who I want to be

I am my own down fall I am my own prosperity.

The path I take in life is my choice and my choice alone.

I have no one else to blame.

—*Author unknown*

Contents

The Beginning

My name is Teresa but everyone calls me T. I've had jet-black hair ever since I was born. My eyes are an emerald green. I was always skinny and wore my hair in a ponytail until I got older. I always wore blue jeans, T-shirts, and Chuck Taylor tennis shoes.

I was told I looked just like my mother when she was my age, but all I ever saw were pictures of her, because I was raised by my uncle. He always wore bib overalls and work boots. Don't think he owned anything else actually because that's all he ever wore. Was never sure what he actually did, but I was raised to never disrespect your elders.

What I'm about to tell you will seem a little crazy, but I can assure it's all true. When I was five, it was the first time I saw the chamber, but I was 12 when I first entered it. That day would ultimately change my life forever. The chamber was always hidden behind two doors in our basement. I was never allowed past the first door.

We lived in an old house in a not so nice neighborhood, but it was all I knew of as home. Other kids would always say I lived on the wrong side of the tracks, but it never bothered me, because I liked my side of the tracks. It was a small house, just like most of the other houses in our neighborhood. My home was a dingy shade of yellow with brown shutters. Our porch was pretty big and wrapped all around the side of the house. The backyard had an old rusted fence around it, but wasn't very big. There was space outback for my uncle to park his old beat-up Ford pickup. I guess he was the local handy man and most of the time didn't charge for a lot of the things he did. Especially for the older neighbors. He'd always say they have it hard enough. His truck used to be red, but now was mostly rust.

We had a small living room with one TV in the house. We only got three channels, since we didn't have cable. My uncle always said if you're that bored, surely there is someone in the neighborhood you could always go help with some chores. I never wanted to be that bored, so at times that's exactly what I did.

There were two bedrooms, both upstairs. I did have my own bathroom, which was rare for where we lived. Mine was in the front of the house and my uncle's was in the back. We had a gym in the attic and I always had to work out with my uncle. "Strong body supports a strong mind," he'd always say. He was strong as an ox.

Our kitchen was small. The cabinets were about the same color as the house. I hated them. Our stove was supposed to be white, but it was so old it looked kind of gray to me. There was a small room in the back where I guess my uncle would pay all our bills. Never went back there much.

We had a basement with pretty much nothing in it, except a washer and dryer that was older than our stove, I think. My uncle would always be working on them. One time he was fixing the washer and the hose busted wide open and sprayed water all over him. It hit him right in the face and he fell backwards over the little stool he was using. I was laughing so hard my belly hurt. When he got up, the look he gave me made me run as fast as I could up the stairs. I could hear him laughing but I didn't dare go back down.

There were two rooms in the back, but I was never allowed back there. We were white and mostly all the other people in our neighborhood were black or Asian. But for the most part, everyone got along and was really friendly.

Our neighborhood had a local store called Andy's Market. It was a small store, but you could get anything you wanted. Sort of like all the little stores before the big chains came in. They wouldn't come here, because it was a very poor area. The owners of our stores would let you run a tab till pay day. My uncle said all the local stores used to do that.

There were several gangs in our area. But for some reason, they stayed away from our area altogether. Uncle

Sam always said it was because of Mama. If they did drive through, it didn't matter what gang it was, they knew Mama would never allow any trouble here. Story goes that years ago, one gang member drove by and shot at Mama's house. I guess they never did find him. Of course, this was just normal to me. Nobody messed with Mama.

Uncle Samuel raised me, when my parents were killed in a car crash just after I was born. My uncle would go away for days on end and Mama would watch over me whenever he was gone. They always treated me like family. Sometimes her sons would start joking and making fun of me about being the only white girl in the neighborhood. Somehow Mama would hear them and walk right out and smack them in the back of the head. One time her oldest took off running and I'll tell you what. For as big as she is, she caught him before he got to the neighbor's house and boy did she give him a whipping. For as big as she was, she was faster that anyone I knew. I always chuckled when she did that.

I was like the daughter she never had. I would help her cook dinner most nights and then take some over to my uncle. He loved Mama's cooking. Every time he left, he would always say, "I'll see you today," which never made sense to me, because it would always be tomorrow.

I finally asked Mama why he always said that. She explained it to me like this, "Every day you wake up, it's today. Have you ever woken up tomorrow?" I said, "No,

I guess not." She says, "That's why he always says *today*. Tomorrow never comes. Always live your life for today, tell those around you how much you love them and care for them." Mama always did that. She said, "Because in the blink of an eye your whole world can change and once it does, it's too late to tell everyone how much you love them. Remember it's always today." I said, "OK, now it makes sense. I guess it's always today."

Mama was a big ole black woman and as nice as ever, as long as you did what you were told. Everyone in the neighborhood knew this, and if you didn't, you would once she branded you. That will all come into play later.

Mama's house was directly across the street from ours. The outside of her house was a dark dingy brown with yellow shutters. Looked like the same person painted both our houses and used the extra to finish the other. And yes, of course, it was my uncle that painted them both. I always said Mama's boys stole ours just to add color to theirs. But she always had a beautiful flower garden in the front and out back. It was like looking at the flowers at Disney World, absolutely beautiful and to watch her four huge sons out there gardening all the time was kind of funny.

Her house wasn't much bigger than ours, but her basement was huge and that's where three of her boys stayed. She didn't have an upstairs, but she wouldn't have walked up the stairs anyway. She had four sons. All were 6' tall and solid muscle. They were always out sitting on her porch. They were like the protectors of our block. If someone they didn't know drove or walked by, they would walk out and see just what they wanted. I mean, they weren't nasty, but just scared the daylights out of you, because they looked like giant walking rhinos coming at you. And, of course, they were always together. Nicest guys ever, but looked mean as ever also. As for Mama, Uncle Sam was even scared of her and he was a big, tall guy. Not sure what he did in the basement, but he never left once he went past the first door.

One day Uncle Sam left the doors unlocked when he heard Mama yelling for help. Funny thing is, it was a giant spider. Her whole family hated spiders. Even her huge sons were scared of them. I knew this was my chance to see what was behind the doors. So I quickly entered and there in the middle of the second room was a solid egg-shaped globe— shiny and really cool-looking. It was about six feet high. There was no door at all, which I thought was odd.

I had to touch it, since it was in my nature to do the opposite of what I was always told. As soon as I put my hands on it, the Egg opened and without hesitation, I entered. It was really neat inside, with what looked like television screens all around and all kind of different-looking symbols all over. There were two grooved-out handles, one on each side. I grabbed them just as my uncle entered the room and yelled NO NO NO several times. The Egg's door closed and I could not let go as the pain throughout my whole body was unbearable. After the pain was gone, I was given visions of all these crazy things about creatures, galaxies, and spaceships. It was truly like watching a *Star Wars* movie about the future.

I was injected with a liquid that was shocking my body and I could see this bright purple entering my veins and running through my whole body. I could see Uncle Sam fighting wars in bits and pieces all over the galaxies. The creatures he was fighting were ugly-looking. They were about nine feet tall and looked like something out of a scary movie. Their ears were small and they really didn't have any nose—just three holes to breathe out of. Their teeth were like fangs and they had large lips. Their neck was big and the rest of their bodies were very muscular like Mama's boys.

I could see other worlds and all types of creatures. This was when I passed out and in the blink of an eye, I woke up in a world like no other. I thought I was dreaming. It was beautiful—vibrant colors of everything you could imagine—rainbows and birds of all colors. Some were very tiny, while some were big as airplanes. Waterfalls with different colored water flowed into one giant body of water like an ocean. Dogs and cats were colored like rainbows and all of them were playing together with many other creatures you would never imagine existed. Yes, unicorns do exist by the way. The rainbows were all different colors just as were all the animals. Some were all one color while others were multiple colors. The ocean that all the waterfalls flowed into was the prettiest color of blue I'd ever seen in the world. All these different colors flowed into it and as soon as they touched the ocean, everything became blue. The ocean was so clear and you could see all kinds of fish and other creatures swimming all over.

There were spaceships that looked like fighter jets, but much cooler-looking and what looked like oblong balloons that were carrying all kinds of different people or things all over the place. The sky was a mixture of colors like light blue, pink, yellow, and purple. Just so beautiful.

All of a sudden, out of nowhere, these huge creatures surrounded me and what looked like a glowing spear was pointed at me. They started speaking this crazy language and were being very forceful. They had muscles on top of muscles and their heads were fairly large dog-like ears standing straight up in the air. For some reason I was not scared, so without hesitation, I answered back in their language, "I am T and I'm from earth. If you touch me, my Uncle Sam will beat you up in a second. And don't even get me started, if I have to tell Mama." I didn't really know what to say. I was scared to death when I was speaking.

The First Meeting

These huge creatures looked at me like I was from Mars, and the expression on their faces was as if I just told them I was their sister—their ears fell down along their head, but that only lasted a second.

That's when I found out they could actually speak English. So they asked me how I came to their world and I started to tell them about how curious I always am. Like when I was six, I wanted to drive my uncle's car, so I took it for a ride just to see. And, yes, I wrecked it into mama's fence and, well, that didn't turn out so well for me. And they responded with, "If you don't get straight to the point, this is not going to turn out so well either. So being me, I laughed and said, "What are you going to do about it?"

That's when one behind me hit me with the glowing stick and the pain at first was unbelievable, but then I'm not sure what happened next, because I just beat up four huge monsters. Next thing I knew, this bubble was around me and I couldn't move. Then I see Uncle Sam standing outside the bubble with this look on his face like if he gets a chance, he is going to wring my neck. Now that's when I was really scared.

Next comes out this amazingly beautiful woman and everyone stopped and bowed down—except me, of course. She looks at Uncle Sam and he turns to her and they walk away. Now she has like twenty of the cutest little creatures walking around her. They had hair like a dog but were round and had these big smiles on their face and three legs and only stood about three feet high. I just wanted to pet one so bad. So my uncle and this beautiful lady walked behind this huge door and it closed.

Well, the creatures were standing outside the bubble. And, boy, were they mad! They were saying as soon as the bubble comes off they are going to teach me a lesson. I was praying Uncle Sam would be out before then. Just as they both came back out, the bubble breaks and these four are about to have me for lunch. Then the beautiful lady yells, "NOCTAR," which somehow I knew meant NEVER. I was going to say something smart, but figured I was already in enough trouble.

They backed off and now Uncle Sam was walking towards me. OK, now I was scared. He looked at me and said, "T, you need to follow me," so we both walked with this beautiful lady and he said, "This is Sheena." She was purple with bright red hair and green eyes that sort of looked like mine. She starts out by saying, "We are on the planet, Nexteria, in the sector of the Planariam galaxy. I will need you to listen to what we're about to tell you."

I asked Uncle Sam if this was a dream and like he always does, he pinched me on the ear and asked, "Does it feel like a dream?"

Boy, did I hate it when he did that. But now I knew this all was a reality. So he begins to tell me about how our ancestors found this egg-shaped thing thousands of years ago. "It has been in the family for centuries, which means forever. We have been tasked with protecting the many galaxies and ensuring that evil never takes hold as it did when your parents were alive."

I said, "I thought you said they died in a car crash."

Uncle Sam said, "No, they died fighting the Quantarians. But you will learn all of this in your teachings."

I said, "What teachings?" he said, "Listen and stop talking."

Sheena sat me down and said, "She was the overseer of all the galaxies. She was tasked with keeping all the different galaxies in harmony and ensuring peace with all the different creatures." Sheena said, "We are all creatures of the Maker."

I asked, "What maker?"

She said, "He is known by many names, but I believe you call him GOD. He created all the worlds that make up the galaxies."

So I asked, "How many galaxies are there, since the Milky Way galaxy is so huge we can't even see past it?

Uncle Sam pinched my ear again and said, "Listen and stop asking questions."

Sheena said, "Now let her ask all the questions she wants."

I looked at him and laughed. I'm glad she was there, because the look on his face was, well, you know—one of those "Wait till we get home" looks.

Anyway, when she waved her hand in the air, the ceiling turned black and all these what looked like millions of stars appeared in the sky. She said, "Each section is a galaxy. The smallest section you see over there is the Milky Way galaxy—it is located on the far end of the systems—the one clear over here is ours, the Planariam galaxy. There are 5,000 different galaxies all with different races and creatures." Then I asked where my parents had died.

She said, "I will explain that to you later. The Quantarians are in control of the Nebula galaxy located clear over in this sector. The surrounding galaxies are our security buffer from them. We have fought many battles with them, as you will see in your lessons ... but that will come with time. Your family has been the protector of all the galaxies and have remained in control of the SECTAR. This is the power source that holds all of our galaxies together in peace. If it were to get into the wrong hands, it would give our enemies power beyond anything we could comprehend. Your training will start immediately. You will now wait outside while I speak to BACTAR.

I asked, "Who is Vatar?"

Sheena looked at me and said, "BACTAR. You do not listen. We will fix that. Now get out."

So, of course, Uncle Sam said, "Now bow and wait outside."

As I bowed, I couldn't help but reach out and pet one of those cute little fur balls. As I did, the smiling little fur ball bit my finger off. I was going to scream, but it didn't hurt at all and then it grew right back. Of course, as curiosity always gets me in trouble, I went to reach down again, but my uncle pinched my ear and said, "Now get out."

Why does he always do that? It really hurts.

Even though I was outside, I could still hear their conversation. Sheena was telling my uncle that I was the chosen one and never has there been a child bearing the sign of the chosen. She said she could feel it. If the marks of Jafar appear, she must be given the SECTAR.

Next thing I remember was my uncle putting his hand around my wrist and waking up in my bed at home. I looked around and wondered if anyone would believe the dream I just had. I walked downstairs and Uncle Sam was having his morning coffee. I said, "Good morning, Uncle." and he looked at me and said "Good morning." I told him I had the craziest dream where I went into the basement back room and entered the Egg and went to this amazing planet and met all these amazing creatures and that he was a warrior for all the galaxies.

He laughed at me and said, "You can call me, BACTAR." That's when my eyes got really big and I passed out. I woke up in his arms and he said, "We have a lot to discuss."

I said, "I can't wait," but he said, "First you will go to school and we'll talk when you get home, but don't tell anyone about anything—you understand?"

I said, "Of course, I understand—just don't pinch my ear, please." So as usual, coming home from school, I would get teased and picked on by these bullies. They picked on everyone, but me especially, because I was white. There were only a few white people in our little school.

Of course, my best friend JT was black and always stuck up for me. We walked to and from school together every day. But today, there were six of them and when JT got in front of me to protect me, they all started beating him up. I yelled, "You punks better stop or you're going to have to deal with me!"

That's when they all stopped and, well, I started running with all six chasing me. I ducked behind the Chin's house and let them pass, then I took off, turned left when I should have turned right, and ended up by the old abandoned house with the locked chain-link fence.

When I turned around, all the bullies were standing there. They started running at me and said, "Let's teach this little girl a lesson she'll never forget." Well, they ended up about the same as the big creatures on Nexteria did. The first one who punched me really got the worst of it. I flipped him upside down and slammed him on the ground.

Then they all tried to grab me, but it was like I was a full-blown karate expert. Every move I did was as if I've been training and fighting for years. It was so smooth and flawless. I didn't even have to think about it. It was so natural. I did a double backflip, grabbed two by the neck, and they passed out. I grabbed each of the other two by the wrist and figured they would wake up on their couch.

The last one ran, but I put my foot on the fence, pushed off and used the side of the house like a wall to leap in front of him. He looked at me and squealed, "Please, don't hit me—just grab my wrist." So I hit him and then grabbed his wrist—just couldn't resist.

I turned around and JT was standing there with his jaw dropped and eyes wide open. He said, "Holy crap!" He never swears, because Mama would kill us if we got caught.

I said, "Let me explain."

Suddenly, Uncle Sam turns the corner and says, "What did I tell you?"

I said, "I didn't tell anyone. They beat up JT for protecting me and then chased me and, well, I have no idea what took over me, but I really kicked some butt." JT agreed.

He grabbed us both by the ear and ordered, "Let's go."

We all sat down at the table and Uncle Sam started to explain what actually happened and what JT saw—that I was being taught martial arts and had been for a long time. JT started laughing and said, "Yeah, right." Uncle Sam grabbed his wrist and, yes, he ended up waking up in his bed. Still not sure how that all works yet.

So Uncle Sam explained that when I use my gifts, he can sense it, because we are connected through the plasma that was injected into my veins when I entered the chamber. I said, "I'm afraid those boys will get more boys and come after me again." He said, "Yeah, like they're going to tell all their friends they got beat up by a girl and need help to get back at her. He actually started laughing out loud and said that in the morning I would begin going into the chamber and start studying all the wars of the past, all the different galaxies, and their inhabitants. I will be trained by the best fighters and understand what is at stake.

He took me to the basement and behind the Egg thing was the back wall. Uncle Sam put his hand in the middle of the wall and it literally disappeared and this huge room opened up. In the middle was a purple orb and hanging in the middle of it was this necklace. He reached in and grabbed the necklace.

He then gave me this necklace with this stone in the middle. It was the prettiest blue with a hint of emerald green in the middle. I said, "What is this."

He said, "This is the SECTAR."

I asked, "But what about the marks?"

He asked me if I had heard all of the conversation and I said yes. I could actually understand all the different languages all the creatures were speaking. But they also spoke English, so I asked him why they did. He said it was more about making your guest comfortable and not making them feel alone. You know how when you walk by some of the Asian kids and they're talking and looking at you—it makes you feel uncomfortable.

I said, "Yes, it does."

"Well, the other worlds try to respect every culture and don't want to make you feel different, so they speak in your language."

"OK, but back to this SECTAR thing and the markings. I don't have any markings."

He said, "Go upstairs into the bathroom and look at your back." So I go into the bathroom and take off my shirt and I screamed—I'm scarred for life. I was looking at this symbol that was being burnt into my skin in different colors, but I felt no pain. This symbol was covering the center of my back. It was like a star you would see in the sky with several points and a blue circle with a green emerald and a red dot in the middle.

I put my shirt on and went back down to the table in the kitchen. I looked at my uncle and said, "Get this thing off me!"

He says, "I can't remove it. No one can remove it. You have been chosen to carry the SECTAR—it's not a choice, but a quest." He goes on to say, "The SECTAR is the true power of the galaxies as a whole. Whoever controls it can control all the galaxies and wield its power, which is unstoppable, and only passed down to those who are chosen by it to hold its power.

"You must never give it up and vow to protect it with your life, if necessary. It will give you the power to defeat any adversary, even when faced with certain death. But the power cannot be abused or used for evil or it will consume you. If it was ever turned over to the wrong people, they could destroy everything.

"But once chosen, it cannot be taken from you. You must gift it to another person as it was gifted to you. However, you must be sure the person is pure and has the sacred mark or it may be used for evil. The Quantarians have been searching for the SECTAR for thousands of years. It has always been hidden from them. They are the most ferocious warriors in the entire galaxy and have been fighting everyone in their search, so they can take over all the galaxies. If that happened, they would be unstoppable.

"The leader of the Quantarians is Kalone. Ever since he has taken over their home planet, it has become a dark and desolate place filled with evil. It used to be a beautiful place like it is here, but he destroyed all of that to take control. He has led them for centuries and took over after killing Bastone, who lead them in peace like all the other galaxies. Kalone killed him and wants to control every galaxy, so he invades different galaxies in search of this weapon you possess. It is a weapon of peace, but in the wrong hands would be the most evil weapon ever concealed. So no matter what, you must never give it up unless the person is marked by the SECTAR. Do you understand the importance of this? It's not about me or you, but everything that exists everywhere."

"Yes," I said, "I do understand. This is who I'm called into battle against when they invade other worlds or when there is an injustice. I have faced Kalone several times, but have never been able to defeat him in battle. Kalone stands about eight feet tall and his arms are as big as my legs. He is solid muscle. He looks like a gorilla in the face, but is bald all over and has two holes on each side for ears. His skin is a grayish-blue and he has sharp teeth like you would see on a vampire in the movies. He always has several warriors called Rekons whose sole job is to protect him. I'm not sure who is actually meaner—them or him—but together they are virtually unstoppable. They are 100 times meaner than the smiling fur balls that bit your finger off."

"Yikes," I said. I asked him why the mark on my back had a red mark in the middle and the necklace didn't.

Uncle Sam said, "The necklace holds the SECTAR and the red dot in the middle of your back is your heart, which is attached to the SECTAR. It is now part of you. We will go over more tomorrow."

Patience in Learning

Uncle Sam informed me, "Every day you will be trained and learn about your new powers. This will start today after school."

"You mean tomorrow, right?" and I laughed.

He said, "You know what I mean, so don't be a smart aleck. Now it is time for bed. Don't worry about JT—he'll think it all was a dream. He won't remember anything and his wounds will be healed by morning."

That night I could barely sleep. I tossed and turned all night. But I was also very excited to see what else I was going to get into. When I closed my eyes, my alarm went off, so I got up, ate the eggs, toast, and bacon, and drank my orange juice. Every day Uncle Sam fixed me a big breakfast. He always said that breakfast was the most important meal of the day.

I walked out the door and JT was there waiting for me as

usual. He looked at me and said, "I had the craziest dream last night." I just started laughing. He said, "What are you laughing at?"

I said, "Just you—so tell me about your dream." So he told me his whole dream, which of course I already knew the whole story. But I had to play dumb and say, "That was a crazy dream, wish I was that tough."

After school we were walking home, when those six boys came walking by and JT says, "Here we go again." But as they quickly walked by, all six looked like they were really beat up. They just looked at us and kept walking. JT just looked at me and somehow he knew that his dream was not a dream at all, but he never said another word about it.

You have to understand—JT and I are best friends, we were both pretty much raised by Mama, and from Day One, we became the best of friends. The first day at Mama's house, I was being cornered by like 50 older kids—OK, so it was only five, but when you're five-years-old, it seems like more. Anyway, JT walked over and knocked all five of them down and said, "This is my friend and you mess with her, you mess with me." At first, I thought he just wanted to kill me himself. But that day, we just played together like we were best friends forever. He was always looking after me and since he was bigger than most boys his age, that always helped.

When I got home, Uncle Sam was waiting for me.

He said, "Are you ready to start?" and I said, "Yes." We walked downstairs into the second room. Uncle Sam sat me down and explained that if anything would happen to the SECTAR, I would no longer be alive, since it is now part of me. It controls all existence, as we know it—it holds everything together. It has been kept on Earth for thousands of years. I asked why it had never left Earth. He explained that Earth has been hidden from the rest of the galaxies since that Time. This is what has kept things safe here. If the Quantarians were to get the SECTAR and use it for evil, it would be the end of everything as we know it. It would give them the ultimate power to control all galaxies. Only once when it was held by a powerful warrior named Maliki was the SECTAR ever in danger of falling into the wrong hands.

You will learn about this later. But the SECTAR has to be given by the chosen one. It can't be taken or it will destroy any and all who would acquire it. So, no matter what would ever happen, you can never give it away, unless it's time for you to pass it on. Sheena would then decide who that would be, if that time ever comes.

So I asked, "Like I could give it to a friend to hold as a joke and see what happens?"

That's when he grabbed my ear and said harshly, "This is not a game. Your whole life will change from this point on." He went on to explain that the room behind the Egg will also be a place I can go and train to hone my fighting skills.

We entered the room again and he shows me this panel on the wall. "When you put your hand on it, you can say any type of training you want to do and the simulator will create it for you. But understand, it is *not* fake, but actual training. You will feel everything as if it is real, to make you stronger and faster and to fight like no other. But you have to *want* to train. Let me show you. So he says, "Bring up a Rekon and Battle T. Full contact." Suddenly, this huge creature appears and punches me square in the chest, so I slam against the other wall. Holy crap, did that hurt!

Uncle Sam orders, "Stop simulation."

I asked, "Did you really have to do that? He said, "Yes, when you call on the simulation, the battle begins immediately—nothing is held back. I want you to understand that."

I said, "I still think you could have just explained that."

He chuckled and answered, "Probably, but I thought it was funny." However, I definitely wasn't laughing. "All your training is up to you."

We walked back to the other room and he put his hand on the Dome. When the door opened, we both entered and the door solidified. The middle panel stores all the languages spoken in the galaxies going back millions of years from all the different cultures—I would learn these as I trained On the right was all the training for combat and all the weapons I could collect and use, if I ever entered into battle.

I stated firmly, "I hope I get to do that." He responded that he hoped not, because he was the one who was chosen to protect the galaxies. Fighting is not a game and should only be used as a last resort.

He said, "Many of us from different sectors are chosen to fight to keep the evil at bay. I hope you are never required to do that. But in the archives, you will see all of this. Behind you is where you can choose what galaxy and planet to travel to. This button here will take you to Nexteria, where you will be doing all your training. A Symphiod named HyJoe will be your trainer.

"But when you are ready to travel, you're never to go left on the panel. That takes you to the Nebula galaxy, where the Quantarians are in control. Their home planet is FOXTERIA and you are to never travel there.

"DO YOU UNDERSTAND THIS?" he asked very sternly—from the look on his face, I knew he was not kidding. So I said, "Yes, but do not pinch my ear—I understand."

Then the front door upstairs opened. You have to understand that in our house, JT was family, so he was welcome anytime. We never knocked at each other's house—we just walked in. JT's mom worked at the local store Andy's

Market and down the street at a little diner. She had two jobs, so he was home alone a lot, but was always over at Mama's most of the time or at our house.

So I asked, '"What's up?" and he answered, "You didn't answer, so I figured I'd just wait till someone showed up." I said I was downstairs and he started laughing and said, "I hope you stayed away from that back door!"

We both laughed, because we knew we were never allowed past the first door. Uncle Sam scared us half to death one day and told us to stay out of there and, well, that was one time we both listened and never ever questioned him on that.

We grabbed two pops and our bikes and headed down to the local playground. We would always ride there and get on the swings and just talk about all kinds of crazy things—what we were going to do on the weekend, where we wanted to live, going to the beach together, where we would like to travel, and everything else under the sun. He said, "I still can't get that weird dream out of my head, it was so real."

I replied, "Yeah, but those punks got what they deserved!"

He said, "How you would know that? I didn't tell you about that."

I said, "Yes you did," and quickly changed the subject. I asked him if he thought we would grow old together and live happily ever after.

He looked like I just punched him in the nose. I quickly said, "As friends, of course."

He said, "Definitely as friends, of course." It was really hard for me, because it was like I was listening to all the conversations around me. I could hear everything. But as soon as I concentrated on our conversation, I was able to tune everyone else out. I really didn't understand what was going on, but I soon would find out.

We rode down to the ice cream store called Henry's Dairy Owl and we both got two huge sundaes. I always ordered extra strawberry ice cream and hot fudge on mine, but JT always ordered extra chocolate with lots of nuts and also extra pineapple. We both loved those. They truly had the best ice cream in the world. Well, in our world anyway.

After that we went back to my house and watched the movie, *Goonies*. We both loved that movie, also. My uncle came upstairs and I could sense something was wrong. He looked at me and although he didn't speak, I could hear him say, "Everything is fine—I'll talk to you tomorrow," and he went to bed.

The movie was over, so JT went home. I couldn't wait for tomorrow to begin. At 5 a.m., Uncle Sam wakes me up and orders, "'Let's go." It was like my alarm must not have gone off.

I said, "Sorry," but he just said, "It's 5 a.m." I was thinking,

Are you crazy? but didn't want my ear pinched first thing, so I got dressed and to the basement I went.

I said, "You know JT will be by at 7:30 to pick me up for school," but he said, "Don't worry about that." He explained that when I'm on pod time, it's not like here—an hour in the pod is just minutes on earth, so people here will think nothing of it when you're gone.

Then he said, "You will train in the mornings before you go to school. This way you will not draw any suspicion to yourself. Once your training is over for the day, you will just concentrate on home and you'll be brought back to the Shell. Yes, the shiny egg-shaped thing is called the Shell." He already knew I was going to ask about that one, so I navigated the control panel to Nexteria.

When we land, it's pretty cool. We are slammed to the surface and we land with one knee on the ground and the other bent and both fists on the ground. Well, to be honest, I landed on my face the first few times. I didn't really think it was funny, but Uncle Sam thought it was—he laughed every time.

We are greeted by HyJoe. He looked like a gentle old frail person, but not human by any means. He had purple skin, his eyes were yellow, he had ears like a dog, and his face was long and thin. His first words were, "Yes, I know what I look like, but you must never judge a book by its cover." When I went to say something, he said, "Yes, I know you're sorry."

After my uncle leaves, HyJoe takes me to this big dome. After we enter and get close to the center, he speaks no words, but tells me to stand here and do not move. He will return soon. At this point, I'm scared and excited all at the same time. He walks out and after I stand there for like forever, I was really thinking he forgot about me. Then all of the sudden, he appears and says that I did very well. Then, he said, "You may go home now. We will train again tomorrow."

I said, "But we didn't do anything!" He responded with, "You did not pay attention. Your first lesson was about discipline and doing what I instructed you to do. You did not move, therefore, you didn't have to be punished."

So I said, "You wouldn't have known I had left."

He said, "Correct, but the huge creatures that came at you the first time I came were all of a sudden all over the room. They had some sort of camouflage and blended in with the room." He said, "You would not have been happy if you had moved. Of course, I told Sheena that they were not allowed to touch me."

HyJoe said, "In the training room, everything is on the table—you are not protected in here, but they learned not to be gentle on you since their last encounter. In time, you will be able to sense when someone or thing is near, but that will come in time. HyJoe said you stood still for 24 of your hours, so I'm very impressed.

So I did what Uncle Sam said and concentrated on home. Within seconds, I was back. JT showed up and we went to school. I fell asleep several times in my chair and once fell clear out of my seat. Everyone was laughing, except me. I ended up in the principal's office. I just told him I didn't sleep good last night and it won't happen again.

Training Day Starts

So that night, I was telling Uncle Sam about how I fell asleep in school and then started to tell him about my first day. He stops me and says, "When you go into the Shell every day, you will need to grab the handles—your body will be given the energy it needs to recharge. Once your training is over, you will only need this when you are totally drained, but that is rarely ever. As for your training, I do not need to know about that. The training is between you and HyJoe. Everyone is trained differently."

I went straight to the basement, grabbed the handles, and my whole body lit up this bright yellow. I felt amazing, so for the next few hours I just started going through all the different symbols. It was confusing at first, as there were panels all over the inside of the Egg. I mean like the screens were all around and you could just swipe and different symbols and icons like on a phone is the best way I can explain it. I could go back in time and see the past and see things current in a split second.

Every creature was color-coded and I could see all the different galaxies and their inhabitants. There were planets covered all over with water and many different creatures swam together. They were all colors, like on Nexteria. Some whale-like creatures were as big as cruise ships, while others were as small as tadpoles and every size in between. Of course, not everyone got along perfectly. It was amazing to swim with all the different species on this planet.

Once all these bigger fish were sort of teasing this little fish. I started to go over, when this huge—and I mean huge—shark swims to one little fish, opens his mouth, and swallows the little fish. Then he swims over to where all the little fish are playing and opens his mouth—that little bugger just swims out of his mouth and to his friends. I just started laughing.

You see, I was able to breathe through my mouth and my ears acted like gills and filtered out the oxygen. Every creature on these planets are able to get whatever their bodies needed either through the air or the water. Truly amazing.

As JT and I are checking out different planets, I took him to Estonia. Now this planet was much different than most. It is literally covered in plants and looks like a huge jungle. The grass was the most beautiful emerald green

you could ever imagine. It was so soft to the touch. How I
know this is because the first time I landed here, I hit face
first—wasn't so funny at the time though. And of course,
JT landed face first, also. That was funny.

Anyway when you first looked around, it seemed like
you could not go through anywhere. But as soon as you
moved, all the bushes, plants, and trees would literally
move out of your way, so you could just go everywhere.

There was no life on this planet like other places. It was
solely inhabited by living things that grew from the planet
itself. Different species could visit, but none stayed. The
plants were all different colors. Some glowed and some
were not as bright, while others were the most vibrant
colors you could ever imagine—blue, red, orange, purple,
green, yellow, pink. The leaves were all different colors but
were the same plant.

Yes, the plants could all speak to each other, also. That's
how I learned that every night the rain would fall and feed
the whole planet. It would all be absorbed by the occu-
pants of the planet. The planet would be dry for the rest
of the day until the nightly rain. I learned that at one time,
the Quantarians attacked the planet to harvest it for food,
but my uncle and others came and fought them, so they
retreated back to their own galaxy. This was told to me
by the Eldest tree there. Said he was the first living thing
placed by the One on this planet. From him I learned that

all planets except Earth received all their nourishment from the water and the air.

Up to this point, I was never really sure how everything survived, because I never saw anyone eat or consume any type of food. It was all provided for them by the Creator. Of course, Earth was not this way, but it was hidden from all the other galaxies.

I just had to share this beautiful place with JT. As we were going leave, the eldest tree said, "You And Your Mate Be Safe." I told him that we were just Best Friends. He said, If You Say So."

Once we were back on Earth, we headed over to our favorite little pizza shop called Iggy's pizza. It was just a little family-owned restaurant and bar, serving the best slice of pizza you could ever ask for. It was literally just around the corner from my house. It wasn't very big inside, but they had a few tables and made the pizza right in front of you. Petty cool. JT was going on and on about our trip. I loved taking him places, because he truly appreciated everything, just like I did. So we ate our pizza and went back home.

One other planet had thousands of flying creatures. Yes, dragons are real, I can assure you. I even rode one! His name was Charlie—yes, Charlie—I know a dragon named Charlie. You really can't make this stuff up. So he flew across their planet so I could see everything. We were high in the sky, then dove straight to the ground, and literally stopped just feet off the ground. I think he was trying to scare me. OK, it did. And all the creatures could speak to each other. It's like I was injected with all this different knowledge about all the cultures. I was given different fighting techniques from all over the 'galaxies. It was like I was doing battle as I ingested every technique. I was trained on all sorts of weaponry.

When I went back to the archives, I could see my uncle in battle with many other cultures throughout time. It was mainly the Quantarians that started the battles trying to take over different planets. I also learned about the gifts each culture was given—it was not all about war and fighting.

I also learned how all cultures interacted with each other, how they loved one another, and all things living and dead. All cultures praised life and embraced their own while alive. They truly cherished life and welcomed death as they knew of the Higher Being. All cultures called this Being by different names, but there was always mention of the true Giver of Life and how He performed miracles on many different levels. Yes, there were people who disbelieved of His existence, but their cultures never judged. We wait to tell people after they pass how we miss them, while they spend life together so they all know in death they are missed.

Most of the planets had no way to defend themselves if ever attacked, but they were mostly peaceful. Now I understood why my uncle and others were always prepared for battle to defend those who couldn't defend themselves. I really couldn't grasp why anyone would ever want to harm so many beautiful creatures. I was always treated like family on every planet I visited in my travels. But I could never tell them where I came from, because I was protecting the SECTAR.

The Shenones were fearless warriors, but bonded at a very young age with one male and one female. They spent their entire life together and in battle never left each other's side. They showed love and compassion for one another and never were ashamed to show it. They never disrespected one another or anyone. When I visited their planet, I was truly amazed how much love and compassion they truly had for every living thing.

They looked a lot like humans, but their body was red and always covered with armor. The males had tails and the females did not. Their eyes were black as coal, their ears looked like gills, and they had very tiny noses. But if disrespected, they would not walk away from battle, but it was only used as a last resort. If one was killed, the other stayed by their side and died beside them, if necessary—sort of reminded me of JT and myself. We were always together. The next day I was dressed and ready when my uncle opened my door. I just said, "Don't ask—I just woke up on my own." I entered the Shell and grabbed the handles just so I wouldn't get tired. I felt so strong and energized. I arrived on Nexteria and went straight to the dome. HyJoe was waiting on me. "Today we start your combat training," he commanded.

In walks five small creatures called Sabors that looked a little like wolves with shaved bodies that were bulging with muscles. They introduced themselves to me and the next thing I knew, I was being tossed to the ground, At first, I was stunned, but I countered that move by sweeping the legs out from under two of them. Immediately, I was struck from behind by one, but when I turned around, the other four attacked me. I was cut and bleeding. HyJoe stepped in and said now heal yourself and start over.

Without even thinking, my body healed itself and it started all over again, except this time, I was better prepared. I fought all five at once and in the end, they got exactly what they gave me the first time. But don't think they gave in—it was one heck of a battle. They were fast and mean. After that session, HyJoe said I needed to learn that even the friendliest creatures may also be the most vicious fighters.

So daily I would go into the training room on earth and learn to fight techniques from all creatures and cultures. Yes, I got beat up a lot. Yes, it was not all fun. I mean I really got beat up bad on some days. But I learned new things every day. Some fighters had compassion and mercy, while others had none. I should have known this from my own neighborhood. Always be on guard.

Back home I went and JT again picked me up. He said, "'What's up? You seem different." I was like, "What are you talking about?"

JT said, "Not sure—just something is different about you." So every chance I could get, I'd go into the Shell to learn and study. I continued my training every day, got stronger every day.

In the archives, I saw all the battles my uncle had fought in. There was nothing glorious about war. Many creatures and species were killed, because one group wanted galaxy domination. Understand, the Quantarians controlled a whole galaxy with hundreds of planets that they had taken over. The hardest part was seeing my parents in battle, and watching how they were killed. They were summoned by the Quantarians for a truce and were ambushed, but they were not alone. There were probably 500 fighters and 30 different spaceships and 100 fighter spacecraft that went with them. It was quite amazing to see. Just like on Nexteria, all their armor was covered in bright colors. Truly beautiful.

After all the troops were on the ground, the ships the Quantarians had surrounding the other ships were four to one. They first fired upon the ships without warning. The battle in the air didn't last long, but they were able to send a message to my parents that they were under attack. That's when the ground battle started. There were fighters from several galaxies with my parents. The battle raged on for hours. They were surrounded by thousands, but no one ever gave up. My parents fought side by side till the very end. They were the last two standing and when my father was killed, my mother went into a wild rage. I'd say she killed another 100 Quantarians before she was killed. But the whole time, she never left my father's side.

I was crying the whole time while seeing this archived battle and mad as ever. I still cry at times, just because I never did get to know them. My uncle who was trained under them took over as protector of all galaxies.

My next day of training, I told HyJoe I wanted to train harder and be the best, so I could get revenge for my parents being murdered. He started to tell me they were cowards and they deserved to die. I was so mad. I challenged him and he beat me like something you could only imagine. No matter what I tried or how hard I tried to hit him, he would smack me so hard, I really couldn't even think straight. Then I'd get even madder and it even got worse for me.

This happened several times. The last time he had his hand on my chest as he slammed me to the ground and told me, "You must never seek revenge, for you lose concentration on your actual skills and will be defeated by your own mistakes."

I said, "But you said things about my parents that weren't true."

"Yes, I know, but I did this to make you so mad you would lose control and make grave mistakes. You knew the truth about your parents, so never let words cause you to react, because they are just words—not the truth. Put this bracelet on and never take it off. The top section when held will give you the swords of GALION, which will be your primary weapons. Hold the bottom and this will notify your uncle and the Council you are in danger."

The bracelet was beautiful—silver with two stones in the center, The top stone was blue like a beautiful light blue sky on earth, while the bottom, was the most beautiful color purple you would see when the sun is setting over the ocean.

Council Meets HyJoe

It is a very rare occurrence when the council is summoned to Nexteria to meet with Sheena, but even rarer for the meeting to be called by HyJoe. The meeting starts off with 5,000 representatives from all the galaxies. As Sheena enters from a hole in the center of the room, everyone and everything bows.

Sheena calls the Council to order. But the first business was not HyJoe, it was from the galaxies surrounding the Nebula galaxy. The Quantarians are massing a force as never seen before. They have been testing our defenses and have attacked several outlying areas and killed many allies—when they attack, they destroy everything. They put up a video captured by some of the fighters that tells us we must act as soon as possible to retaliate, before they can advance into our outlying galaxies.

The Quantarians have converted several hundred

thousand other warriors with their mind machine. We have never seen them this strong. After watching more battles, the Council agrees something must be done.

Sheena asked for a vote to gather an army to defend the outer regions and squash the Quantarians from advancing. The vote is unanimous—every galaxy agrees to send thousands of warriors and ships for the battle. Actions are put into play and the army will advance to the region as soon as everyone can be mobilized.

Next order of business was HyJoe. He starts out by referring back in history to when the SECTAR was in the hands of the chosen one, Maliki. He was one of the fiercest warriors and with the SECTAR by his side, he was unable to be defeated. His fighting skills were unmatched by any, until the one battle when he faced Kalone, who was also one of the fiercest warriors and feared by all. Until this day, Kalone was always able to escape Maliki in battle. But what we didn't know was Kalone had traveled to the dark side of good and evil and acquired the Ring of SALINE, which was thought to be a myth. This ring gave him extraordinary powers, so in the fiercest battle, he killed Maliki, but when he reached for the SECTAR, BACTAR grabbed it from his neck and brought it here. Which is why, to this day, its exact location has been hidden.

HyJoe continues, "Well, I'm here to tell you I have been training LUC over the past several years. She has become the most advanced warrior I have ever trained. She came to us from far away as a child. I have taught her all I know, so now she has been teaching me."

Many Council members start talking, saying that they would put their best warriors against this LUC. HyJoe ran some of the training archives and they all just stared at the giant screen on the ceiling. LUC had defeated all their warriors and not just one on one, but even 50 on one."

HyJoe says, "I tell you this, because if the Quantarians do start to take over again, we may have to call on her."

The Council all yells, "Vote, vote, vote .... Sheena stands and yells, "NOCTAR!"

Then she speaks, "I have been chosen by the SECTAR to be its protector. I will not allow the SECTAR to fall into the hands of the Quantarians. If that happens they would have the power to control everything. The Council does not object, because they all know the SECTAR must be kept out of the hands of evil."

Now BACTAR had been silent, because he knows that I have advanced far beyond any training he could imagine. He agrees to lead the army to the outlying galaxies and engage the Quantarians. He knows they must be stopped at any cost. So as the Council is dismissed and all agree that the army will assemble and leave within the next several weeks.

Now Uncle Sam (BACTAR) requests to meet with

Sheena and HyJoe about me and the request is granted. He is upset that he was never informed about how advanced my training had become.

HyJoe explained that LUC aka T (me) had progressed at a rate never seen before. The last creature to be this good was Maliki and LUC surpassed him within the first few years of her training. She has skills that can't be taught and since she has been trained, no one has beaten her in battle. Her body recovers instantly and her cells reproduce at a rate at the speed of light. I have sensed she has seen battle, but she has the ability to block all her thoughts—even to the seer's. She must not meet the Quantarians in battle. They all agreed that the SECTAR must be protected at any costs.

Now of course, I'm not 12 anymore and I'll be graduating high school soon. JT and I have been best of friends from the start. We have this connection that just can't be broken. Neither one of us has a boyfriend or girlfriend, because every time we tried, that person always says that our friendship has to be broken'. And, well, we agreed never to let that happen.

Uncle Sam returns home and sits me down. He says, "Tomorrow I want to go train with you." I said OK, but felt really funny about that. The next day, we go to Nexteria and enter the dome together. The look on HyJoe's face was, *Holy crap—this can't be good.*

So HyJoe and BACTAR have a little discussion and BACTAR says, "I need to know how good she *really* is." HyJoe says, "I would not recommend that, but it's up to you."

Uncle Sam looks at me and says, "Today we fight, I'm not your uncle and today you will fall." At first I thought he was joking. As I turned my head to look at HyJoe, BACTAR punched me as hard as he could in the chest. I flew across the room and slammed into the other side of the dome. The whole dome shook like an earthquake had hit it. Then he was right in front of me and slammed me into the ground. I'm thinking, *I can't fight my uncle.*

Then he pulls out a BASTON, which is a long glowing stick, which can be deadly if driven through an enemy's chest. I activated my swords and we fought like forever until I realized he really was trying to test or kill me—at this point, I wasn't really sure. He had already hit me several times and I had healed myself.

I looked at him and said, "Today you are not my uncle—you are my enemy." He said, "Correct. Now fight."

But now I was done playing. Within seconds he was on his back and I had my sword against his throat. He knew now how well I could fight. He stood up and said, "I'm very proud of you."

What he didn't know is I had been going into the simulator every day and training—I actually loved it. At first, it was not fun, because I truly got the crap beaten out of me daily—I mean, for months. But then I started to get stronger by using the different fighting techniques I learned in the SHELL.

He said, "Tomorrow we must talk." I said, "I know."

We headed back to earth. JT still picked me up for school so off we went. He could tell something was wrong and asked me about it, but I said nothing. I could tell he didn't believe me. After school we went to the movies and when he dropped me off, Uncle Sam was waiting up for me. Our talk was about to start.

The Talk

As we sit down for breakfast, Uncle Sam says, "There's a lot we need to go over." Just then the front door opens and JT walks in. Uncle Sam gets right up and meets him before he gets three steps into the house and says, "T is sick and not going to school today. Call her later to see how she's feeling.

As JT leaves, Uncle Sam starts to tell me that the bracelet on his arm is actually an emergency beacon. It's sort of like the one I have, except his was given to him by the Council and because he has fought for so many different galaxies, when and if ever needed, he could just wrap his other hand around his bracelet and it would summon all and let them know that he is in imminent danger and needs help immediately. He has never needed to use it and hopes it stays that way.

He asked me if I have ever seen real combat other than

the training or in the archives. I felt I had to lie to him and tell him no. He said be honest and again I said no. I have never lied to him, but didn't know how to tell him what happened to JT and me. I'll explain that later.

He says Kalone has collected the Quantarians and has been attacking the outer galaxies with a massive force. He has acquired the Ring of SALINE, which is like the SECTAR, but not as strong. It has long been hidden, but somehow he has obtained it. With his new power, we fear he can start taking over the galaxies at will. The Council has decided to attack him before he can advance.

Uncle Sam said he may be gone for several days or weeks. At this point, I knew things were getting serious, because he was usually gone only a few hours a day at any given time. However, I remembered with the time difference that weeks are months here on earth.

I asked how come Earth has been able to stay so safe from all this fighting that has been going on for CENTARS. He explained that earth has been shielded by the Planariam galaxy and what we see from here has always been protected by Nexteria. It is like a giant mirror with a reflection facing outward. If you saw a screen that showed all the 'galaxies, Earth is located on the far edge. What people here see is actually controlled by Nexteria. Probes that are launched by our NASA are actually hit with a beam once they get so far out. But it's not a malfunction as most here think.

That's why the SECTAR was given to us here on earth—especially now that Kalone has the ring.

"And another thing, if something should happen to me, you must not seek revenge. I pray you never have to experience what I have."

I said, "BACTAR, I have watched all the archives. I have not gone through what you have, but I have seen everything. I don't fear battle or the Quantarians."

BACTAR says, "Neither do I, but I do respect that they are fierce warriors and train for battle every day. You have to understand, when they are born they start training to fight. If they can't fight, they are taken to the mines and worked until they die."

So then he asked me, "How come HyJoe calls you LUC?" I explain that every time in training someone would get a hold of me, I would squirm my way loose. No matter what. So every opponent when we got done would ask, "How did you get loose?" I'd always say, "Because you are weak." They would get mad and grab me and 'I'd get loose again. So HyJoe started calling me LUC. I liked it."

BACTAR says, "I am being summoned and must leave immediately."

I replied, "I know. And please be careful, the Quantarians have taken over the outer galaxies and are advancing at a rapid pace."

He looked at me and said, "How do you know this?" I

explained, "I can hear anything I want—it's amazing. The Council has just gotten word of the attacks, so you must go now."

He said one other thing before he left, "I have unlocked the archives to a secret file and once I leave you must open it and watch." I promised I would, so Uncle Sam goes to the basement and leaves. Just then, JT shows up and says, "OK, what's going on? I know you never get sick."

The Day That
ALL Would Change

So back to Mama. As I said, Mama was the funniest cool-est mom on the block. She was like a stepmother to every kid in the neighborhood. Now when I say she branded me when I wrecked into her fence, this is what happened. After I hit her fence, I was called into her house. She always had something cooking on the stove, because she fed all the neighborhood kids. No one went hungry around Mamas house. I mean no one.

But when you messed up, she would smack you on the back with one of those pans and it actually burnt your skin and now you had Made in the USA across your back. God only knows how many people she did that to, but then it was like you were a blood relative. Mama would protect you with her own life if she had to.

And Mama was very religious—every time she fed you, she made you bow your head and pray and thank God for protecting us and putting food on our table. One day, one of the fathers going to work told Mama he didn't believe God created everything. He went through the whole evolution thing and said the Big Bang started it all. Mama looks at him and said, "OK, then I say God created the Big Bang, so in the end, he created all."

He replies, "I don't get it," So she invites him. We could hear him scream. We knew what happened. Next thing we know, he says, "OK, I believe." We all laughed when he left with his back steaming. We knew he just got the Made in the USA welcome to the neighborhood. I had to laugh when Uncle Sam and I were fighting, because he had the same thing on his back. That's just part of living in our neighborhood.

Like I said earlier, Mama was about 5'5" tall and weighed an easy 400 pounds. If you asked, she'd say, "Ask again and you'll find out." We always laughed. Boy, oh boy, could she cook though. I basically lived there whenever Uncle Sam was away. Of course, now I know that she knew exactly what Uncle Sam was and what he did. But still no one ever messed with her.

Because I was able to go into the shell and travel and with all the knowledge and powers I was given, I could block anyone's view of what I was doing or where I was headed. But of course, I just traveled to the safe zones as BACTAR has instructed me.

The little furry creatures that protected Sheena were called Typhons—their planet was almost destroyed by the Quantarians. Then BACTAR came in and defeated them, so they have pledged always to be there if he needed them. The same thing happened to the Shenones. BACTAR fought side by side with them against Kalone and made him retreat, even though they took major losses. The Shenones also pledged their life if ever needed. He had so many galaxies that thanked him for all the battles he had fought, I could never see him ever being defeated, unless of course I was fighting him. I just made myself laugh.

One day when I was sixteen, I was so excited about looking into the archives, because from watching Uncle Sam fight, I learned what to do and what not to do. Yes, I'm still learning things daily.

Anyway, back to that day I left the doors open, I was facing the back of the Shell from inside. Little did I know JT had come in the house earlier and was hiding in the basement. As I entered, JT came running behind me and pushed me in. As he did, my hand went across the left side of the panel and the next thing I knew, we were being slammed into the ground on a dark and dreary planet.

At first I laughed, because I landed perfect and JT slammed face first into the sand on this cold dark planet.

I laughed so hard my stomach hurt. The look on his face was like he just pooped his pants in front of the whole class. He yelled, "What in the heck just happened? You look like you just got yelled at by Mama and was about to get smacked."

That's when I realized I had just transported us to the Nebula galaxy and we had landed on Kalone's home planet, Foxteria. The planet was dark and dreary, with sharp rocks all over and very cold. I knew we should go back to Earth, but I couldn't help wanting to look around. I mean, I'm sure I would never get to see this again. So when JT wanted to know what had happened, I said, "Just shut up and don't say anything—I'll explain later," he was speechless.

There was black sand all over this world, but once you got off the sand, it was like walking on sharp little rocks and they crunched every time you stepped—like stepping on ice crystals. As we walked around this big rock formation, we could see lights down in the valley below us, but it was more like fire on sticks than actual lights. It was one of the mines I was told about.

The soldiers on guard were beating the workers every time they messed up—and from what I could tell—even if they didn't mess up. I'm not sure what they were mining, but it looked a lot like coal. We started to go further to see what looked like a huge city. It was barely lit up and most of the structures were a light gray. On the one side, we saw what looked like massive army training and these crazy-looking spaceships. I felt very uncomfortable, so I whispered to TJ, '"Let's get out of here."

We walked on the side of another hill and I could see Rekons coming our way. I looked at JT and said, "Hide over here." JT yells, "I'm tired of you telling me what to do!" I was about to ring his neck, but the next thing I knew, the Rekons were surrounding us. There were at least ten of them.

At first they were speaking in their native language, which sort of sounded like a grumbling old man's voice. I yelled back at them, "I am LUC."

They just stared at me at first. Then JT says, "What the heck—is this a dream?" I just told him to shut up, because I knew we were in bigger trouble when they started speaking our language. They commanded a solider to summon Kalone, saying, "The SECTAR is here."

They asked us, "Where are you from?" Like an idiot, JT in this scared voice says, "Earth." I quickly pushed JT aside and told him not to move. They were warriors like I'd never seen. They fought like they had trained their whole life, because they had.

The battle lasted about 15 minutes. After they were defeated, I grabbed JT and concentrated on getting home. At the same time, I realized one of them had gotten away to get Kalone. I was scared to death and JT looked white like a ghost—I do mean white.

Once back on Earth, I grabbed his wrist to erase his memory of this, but somehow I couldn't erase what happened to us—because he had gone through the Shell. So I opened the Shell and he tried running up the stairs. I grabbed a rope hanging on the wall and lassoed his leg and dragged him back down the steps. I grabbed him, pinched his ear, and said, "Listen, sit down and I'll explain everything."

"He said, "Pinch me again—I'm dreaming, right?" I said, "No," so I started from the beginning and explained everything from Day One.

He said, "I think I'm going to be sick—I have to go home." I looked at him and said, "You can't tell anyone."

He said, "Are you nuts? Who would believe anything you just told me, let alone what I just saw." Then he ran off.

Over the next few years, JT would go into the chamber with me when I was looking at the archives. I was able to sneak him into Nexteria to see the stunning planet and all the creatures. He was truly amazed at all the beauty, just as I was. I just wished I could take him every time I went, but this was not allowed. So now, JT is with me as I open the file Uncle Sam had given me. Here were my parents explaining that if anything ever happened to them, their son, Sam, was not to tell his sister, Teresa, the truth. From that day on, he would erase her memory and pose as her uncle—not her brother. Boy, was I mad as ever. All this time, I always wanted a brother and I actually had one! When I see him again, I'm going to kill him—well, not really, but I was really, really mad.

The Battle Begins

Because I control the SECTAR, I can't go to my uncle (my brother, really). I can tap into the Shell and see the battle as it is unfolding. The council has amassed a huge army. There was one hundred thousand or more, the largest ever seen in the galaxy. My brother leads the first wave and the fighting is fierce.

The Quantarians have these Sabor fighters that are like triangle-shaped spaceships—the same ones we saw on Foxteria—there are thousands of them. But the Council had their own fighter jets, aka spaceships, that looked cool as heck. They were all bright colors: blues, orange, purple, bright green. They were shaped sort of like our fighter jets, but more rounded all over. In battle, their wings would sweep back into the spaceship, so they could move faster and maneuver quicker. Man, were they cool-looking.

Anyway, the air battle was the craziest thing I'd ever

seen—like watching a *Star Wars* movie, but for real. The ground war starts as soon as the air war begins. IT was sad to actually watch, knowing this is real and going on now, and my brother is leading the ground war. Both sides were taking heavy casualties. But for some reason, the Quantarians didn't seem to have the numbers fighting for them that they claimed to be massing. This perplexed BACTAR and the others. Why would they not be here fighting in force? Something is definitely wrong—I mean we were in the Shell for a good 24 hours and never left. But what we couldn't understand is why the Shell was blinking this red light above our head the whole time. But soon we would know why.

The fighting continues and all of a sudden, JT who went upstairs to get something to eat comes down and says, "T you better get up here."

I said, "Shut up, I'm watching the battle." He says, "I think we have a battle of our own here," but I thought he was joking. He yells, "I mean **NOW!**" in this high, screeching voice.

So I leave the Shell with some reluctance and walk outside. The sky was dark and these huge ships covered the sky. I knew exactly what was happening now—I'd been found. How, oh how did the Quantarians find Earth? How could they get here and yet, I didn't sense it? I thought it was hidden and protected. Then it dawned on me—I had lied to my brother about traveling to other planets. But still, how did they find me? By traveling to their planet from here, they were able to track me. This is all my fault.

Of course, the earth was still hidden and that's why it took them so long to track me down and then set their plan in place. They would gather a force and send out signals saying their whole Armageddon would be attacking the outer galaxies. But this was all to draw the armies of all the galaxies to the outer areas and they would be so consumed with stopping him, they wouldn't expect him to actually bring most of his forces through a wormhole and attack Earth to control the SECTAR.

As soon as he enters the earth's galaxy, the world would react. Even though we all don't get along like the other galaxies, we would have to come together. At NASA, they first see a giant blimp entering from deep space. Of course, we don't have the weapons other worlds have, but we do have space stations far out that send out small craft that looked like mini-space shuttles to investigate.

As they get closer, they send the signal back showing this massive group of spaceships coming at them. They make contact and the response is a plasma beam that destroys the ship and then the space station. Next there are several thousand fighter spaceships released from the other massive motherships.

From NASA, they see this one giant blob turn into

thirty giant motherships and all these other tiny crafts exiting and surrounding the Armada. The call goes out, as all the nations are now picking this up. The Armada is advancing at an unseen pace. Everyone starts to mobilize forces and are joining the United States to engage this massive threat. The Quantarians massed over the Atlantic Ocean.

Of course the coalition forces figured this was to their advantage, since now they could surround them on all sides and end this as quickly as possible. As they engaged in air combat with the Quantarians, it is quickly found out that out that our weaponry is no match for theirs. The air battle was fierce, but we could not keep up with them in battle. They wiped our aircraft out of the sky like an electric insect zapper. The remaining planes are called back.

On the ground, the United Forces engaged them in battle as they landed. This was more effective, but there was just too many for them to fight. Most are ordered to fall back to plan a second attack, but causalities are high.

The next thing I know, Kalone and about 1,000 Rekons are standing in the street. Kalone looks at me says, "Give me the SECTAR and no harm will come to Earth. Your defenses are no match for us and you have no army as I do."

Now I know I can't give it to him—I know he can't be trusted. Mama comes out on the porch and yells for her boys. Now Mama's boys are about 6'6" and solid muscle.

There are four of them. She says, "Boys, teach these goofy-looking aliens a lesson."

But with one sweep of his hand, Kalone knocks them across the street and into a van parked there. It was like four rhino's hitting it. I can see his ring glowing bright red. I had felt untouchable until now. I'm really starting to get scared.

JT yells, "Call your uncle." I forgot about the bracelet. When I press both the top and bottom buttons of the bracelet, my swords appear and I summon the Council and my brother. I remember my training and tell everyone to step aside. JT stands right beside me and says, "You will have to go through me first you ugly-looking buffoon."

I look at JT and say, "Are you serious?" He says, "If you are going to fight, I'll be right by your side—just like when we fought the Shenones."

Kalone replies, "Then you will die together just as they did." Now JT also went into the training room with me. He had become a great fighter, but this was going to get real ugly fast. Kalone says he will destroy anyone who gets in his way.

Now everyone in the neighborhood is out. When word spreads that Mama's boys are hurt, it was like someone said "Free food for everyone." I mean, all the gangs in the neighborhoods, young and old alike—everyone came out. In our neighborhood, you hurt family, you have to deal with the whole family. They were standing side-by-side with all their differences set aside. There was even a white gang and we're still not sure where they came from—we really didn't care—we would need all the help we could get. They were all watching TV and seeing what was unfolding, so they came to fight. Word spread about Mama's boys getting hurt. I again tell everyone to watch out, as they look scared and mad all at the same time.

I go to engage Kalone, but he disappears behind the Rekons, so I start engaging them in battle. They cannot get ahold of the SECTAR at any cost. Everyone is just watching in amazement until I am caught off guard and get slammed to the ground. I'm bleeding and my body is healing itself as quickly as it can. About one dozen Rekons now jump on me. Then everyone sees I'm going to need help and, well, now the war is on. I mean there had to be a thousand people or more show up on our block. Everyone is fighting them now. Believe it or not, even the military shows up and we are actually holding our own at first.

There are people fighting with sticks, guns, knives, and just using their fists. The battle seems to be going on forever, but there are just too many of them. It seems like for every hundred I kill, hundreds more show up.

My uncle gets the summons from the Council, just as the battle is ending on Foxteria. He knows he must go to Nexteria first to get the re-enforcements gathered, if I'm truly in trouble, because he told me I was to never call him unless it meant life or death—more like death in this case.

BACTAR arrives on Nexteria to find Sheena surrounded by Rekons. He looks perplexed and demands, "What is going on here?"

Sheena says, "The Quantarians are on earth and in control of the SECTAR. If we surrender now, they will spare us and not destroy all the galaxies."

BACTAR yells out, "You know, they will never let us live in peace." He also knows I would never give up the SECTAR.

Again back on Earth in battle, I hit the bottom of the bracelet. Still no BACTAR.

Back on Nexteria, BACTAR say, "LUC is calling for help."

Sheena says, "We know she has engaged the Rekons. She can't defeat them. Kalone has the ring and will destroy her."

BACTAR yells, "WE MUST HELP HER!"

Sheena shouts, "NO, The Council has spoken. She will not be spared!"

BACTAR pleads, "'That's my sister—if she dies, I will die with her."

Again, Sheena states, "The COUNCIL has spoken."

BACTAR shouts, "Who will join me?" No one answered. BACTAR activates his Bastone and kills the

Rekons surrounding Sheena. He yells out, "My sister will not die alone!" He looks at them sadly and says, "I have defended your galaxies for years, but in my time of need, you now abandon me?" And he transports himself to Earth.

The Victors

Little did BACTAR know that I wasn't alone. The whole neighborhood was fighting with me. Even Mr. and Mrs. Chin came out to fight. They were probably seventy-five years old. But let me tell you, they were martial arts experts and were kicking butt all over the street. As he arrived, we start fighting together.

BACTAR says, "We are alone in this."

I said, "No, every one of our family here is fighting with us. It was like a piece of machinery. We were fighting side by side, brother and sister. Kalone was still hiding. I needed to find him to end it all. Two Rekons chase Mama into the house—not good for them at all. You hear all kind of screaming and yelling, but it's not from Mama.

The next thing I know, Kalone has grabbed ahold of my brother with his ring against BACTAR's chest. I can see the pain in my brother's eyes. Kalone yells, "The Council has turned against you. I will spare Earth, if you give me the SECTAR and spare BACTAR."

I looked at my brother and asked, "Is it true?

He said, "Yes, we are alone, so run! He can't get the SECTAR."

I replied, "I will not leave you."

Just then Kalone drives his ring into my brother's chest and the life just leaves his body. I run to him in tears. I remembered his bracelet and wrap my hand around it. Nothing—no one is coming. I look at Kalone and say, "That was the biggest mistake of your life."

I engaged Kalone out of pure rage. But he seems to be getting the best of me, even though I did wound him several times. Then I remembered what HyJoe had taught me in training. I was in such a rage, I was beating myself. Kalone counted on this. So without thinking what happens next takes everyone's breath away? I figure if BACTAR is truly the greatest warrior, if I give him the SECTAR with my heart and soul, maybe he can save Earth and defeat Kalone. If not, Earth will be destroyed.

I grab the SECTAR, reach into my chest, and take my heart and soul. It's actually glowing and I could see it in my hand still pumping. I drive it straight into BACTAR's chest. As I pass over, I whisper, "I love you, brother."

Everyone was in awe. My brother awakens and realizes what I have done. He cradles my lifeless body crying. Mama is bawling her eyes out, which no one has ever seen her do. Now the crazy thing was, I could see everything going on. It was like I was floating around everywhere.

Realizing he has the SECTAR, he stands and faces Kalone. Today we end it all.

Kalone declares, "You can't defeat all my warriors and me. You will perish."

"Then I will die with my sister."

Everyone around, including Mama's boys are now awake and say, "You will have to kill the whole family." Kalone says, "Your family is dead, I killed your parents, your sister, and now you will die."

Now everyone around yells, "We are his family.

Kalone says, "Then I will kill all of you."

All of a sudden, there are tens of thousands of Rekons, and out of nowhere HyJoe shows up beside BACTAR saying, "We have witnessed the ultimate sacrifice. I have brought some friends. We are sorry we faltered. Please forgive us."

Hundreds of thousands of Shenones, Sabors, and Typhons appeared. Now, of course, everyone from Earth was looking like they just saw a ghost. I think they may have thought, *We are in big trouble, because we can't beat all of these crazy-looking creatures.* They had no idea they would be fighting with these creatures.

Within the first engagement, they destroy most of the

Quantarians and the Rekons. BACTAR and Kalone are engaged in one of the fiercest battles anyone has ever seen. They slam each other into houses, cars, and to the ground. All the warriors surround them as they continue to fight. After BACTAR grabs my sword, he soon has Kalone on the ground. He says, "Surrender and you shall live."

KALONE says, "If I live, you will die."

BACTOR drives the sword into Kalone's chest Then he comes over to my body and says, "I would give everything up to have you back—everything." Tears are rolling down his face.

He looks to the heaven's and says, "Mother and Father, I have failed you." There is a long pause. Everyone is crying knowing that I had just sacrificed my life for all of them. My own life.

JT is bawling like a little baby. I wish at this point I could have told JT how I actually felt about him. Sheena appears and says, "You can only give one life. You gave yours a long time ago."

You see, a long time ago in a fierce battle, the King and Queen of the Shenones were in battle, where the Queen was killed by Kalone. BACTAR pledged his life to bring her back as I did for my brother. Please forgive me for not joining you in battle as you have always done for us. This will never happen again.

All of a sudden, out of the sky an image appears. Some

call him God, Buddha, and by many other names. Everyone bows. All knew he existed, but few have ever seen him. He bends down and places his hand over my chest and takes the SECTAR from BACTAR and places it around my neck. He says, "I hope this brings peace to everyone everywhere. There is so much love to be given. There is no place for hate in this world."

He says, "'I am the True Giver of life. She selflessly gave her life on the chance that you all may live. For this, I give her life. That is exactly what he had done for my brother for his selfless act. And out of nowhere, I awoke. It was like I was awake the whole time. I asked my brother what the Savior looked like and he told me, Morgan Freeman, whoever that was.

Next, two Rekons are dragged out by Mama and, yes, they had "Made in the USA" burnt into their backs. When everyone turned around to look for the Savior, he was gone. Everyone there had "Made in the USA" on their backs. We're all family here. And we fought as one. Even a young two-year-old had the mark. We all just laughed.

Mama had the biggest block party ever. Everyone showed up and not one person got into even an argument. Peace was brought back to the galaxies. Many of the Quantarians did escape, but they will be hunted down. Earth will be forever changed from this day forward. We will never look at things the same again, knowing we are truly not alone and that our technology is far behind all others.

So remember, *in the blink of an eye* your whole life will pass. Before you know it, everything has passed. So cherish the living and pray for the dead. For one day, we will all be together.

Review

What did you think of the main character, TERESA (T)?

_____

_____

_____

_____

_____

What would you change about TERESA?

_____

_____

_____

_____

_____

Did you like the character JT?

□ yes   □ no

What would you change about JT?

_____

_____

_____

_____

_____

Did you like the planets Teresa visited?

□ yes   □ no

What was your favorite planet and why did you like it so much?

_____

_____

_____

_____

_____

_____

_____

_____

Which three characters did you like the most and why?

1.)_____

_____

_____

2.)_____

_____

_____

3.)_____

_____

_____

What did you find most interesting about the book?

_____

_____

_____

What did you not like about the book?

_____

_____

_____

Did you like the ending of the book?

❏ yes   ❏ no

What would you change about the ending?

_____

_____

_____

What other creatures do you imagine would have been on some of the planets?

_____

_____

_____

What questions do want to ask the author?

_____

_____

_____

_____

_____

_____

_____

CPSIA information can be obtained
at www.ICGtesting.com
Printed in the USA
FFHW02n0411131018
48774027-52887FF

9 781614 935